Christmas Adventu
in Hazelnut Wood

Written & Illustrated by Peggy Burton

© THE MEDICI SOCIETY LTD · LONDON · 1993. Printed in England. ISBN 0 85503 175 1

It was Christmas Eve and snow was falling. Bobby and Betty Rabbit were on their way to Daisy Duck's shop on the edge of Hazelnut Wood, to help their Mother and Father prepare for Christmas Day. They had invited the Squirrel family to join them.

Daisy Duck's shop was filled with decorations and fancy goods and the rabbits gazed excitedly at the array.

'Good morning,' said Daisy Duck. 'What can I do for you?'

Betty explained that they were having visitors for Christmas and handed her their shopping list. Daisy looked at it, filled their baskets with goodies and wished them a Happy Christmas.

'Happy Christmas Daisy,' they replied, and scurried home again through the falling snow.

Christmas Day arrived and Simon and Sally Squirrel set out excitedly with their Mother and Father to visit the Rabbit family.

As they were nearing the Rabbits' home a snowball flew out of the bushes and hit Simon right on the nose.

SMACK!

And then another, THUD!

'Stop that!' said Simon, guessing it would be Bobby Rabbit. 'I am carrying the Christmas parcels.'

'Is there one for me?' asked Bobby.

'Not unless you stop throwing snowballs,' came the reply as he hurled one back.

Then the two girls started throwing snowballs at each other until Mr Rabbit, who had come out to greet Mr and Mrs Squirrel, called to them all to come inside and get warm and dry.

After opening their presents and eating their Christmas lunch Mr Rabbit told the young ones to put on some warm clothes again because he had an exciting proposal …

A TREASURE HUNT!

'The first clue is a little rhyme which will tell you where to find the second clue,' explained Mr Rabbit. 'This will lead you to the third and if you find your way to the sixth and final clue before dark, you will find some treasure.'

They were all very excited and cried 'Hooray!' None of them had taken part in a treasure hunt before.

Mr Rabbit gave the first clue to Mr Squirrel who was going to go with the children. It read:

> 'Tu-Whit, Tu-Whoo, Tu-Whit, Tu-Whoo
> "He" will show you what to do.'

'That's easy,' said Simon Squirrel. '"He" must be old Mr Owl.'

Bobby led the way to Mr Owl's oak tree.

'Look!' he pointed. 'There is a note on the door.'

Simon quickly climbed the tree to find a piece of paper. To his dismay, it read: 'NOT AT HOME'

'Oh dear, it can't be Mr Owl,' he said.

'What about our friend Olly Owl?' suggested Sally Squirrel.

'Olly! Olly!' she called.

They found Olly perched up in his tree looking very festive in a Christmas hat. Sure enough, in his beak was a piece of paper which read:

'A squashed black hat and a long carrot nose
He's all in white from his head to his toes.'

'Thank you Olly,' Sally said. 'Have a very Happy Christmas!'

They all wondered who
the mysterious person in white could be
and thought hard about how to find the next clue.

As they stumbled through a dip in the wood they heard
a squeak, then 'help!'

Two little heads appeared above the snow.

'What are you doing by yourselves in the snow?' asked Mr Squirrel as they all rushed to help the two half buried mice.

'We have lost our Mother and Father and are c c c cold,' one of them said.

'What are your names?' asked Mr Squirrel.

'I am Tommy and this is my sister Tilly,' said the older one.

Mr Squirrel picked up little Tilly Mouse and put her on his shoulders.

'Can you see your Mother and Father from up here Tilly?'

'No,' she squeaked. 'But I can see a big white snowman with a red carrot nose.'

'Clever Tilly,' they all cried.

Sure enough, the next clue was in the snowman's hat:

'You will find a friend beneath the snow
Where prickles and red berries grow.'

'Lots of people in the forest live under the snow,' said Simon. 'This could be anybody.'

'Perhaps it's Harry Hedgehog,' suggested Betty Rabbit.

But Bobby shouted 'I know who it is!' He ran off towards some holly bushes and brushed away some snow to reveal a sign saying HOLLY LODGE. Bobby knocked and their friend Mr Mole answered. He handed Bobby the third clue with a big smile and a cheerful 'Happy Christmas!'

They were closer to finding the final clue and they all strained their necks to read the note in Bobby's hand. The sun was beginning to go down below the tops of the trees and they knew they had to be quick.

'Above a slippery icy place
You'll find another clue to trace.'

'Right,' said Mr Squirrel. 'Off to the stream.'

15

The stream had been frozen for weeks now, and the animals knew very well how slippery and icy it was.

In the branches of a tree overhanging the stream they saw a piece of paper fluttering in the chilly breeze.

'That must be the clue,' said Simon, quickly running up the tree and jumping onto the branch.

'Be careful,' said Mr Squirrel, but Simon had already shaken the tree and a big dollop of snow fell on top of him as the clue floated downwards.

'I'll get it,' said Tommy Mouse and before Mr Squirrel could stop him he slid along the ice, picked it up and read it in his squeaky voice:

'Among the nut trees will be best
To find the clue to the treasure chest.'

They searched and searched among the nut trees but couldn't find the last clue.

It was beginning to get dark and the air was growing cold, when suddenly Tilly heard something.

'Listen,' she said. They all stopped and stood very still.

'Tommy, Tilly, where are you?' someone called.

It was Mr and Mrs Mouse.

The mice dashed off to meet them and tell them about the Treasure Hunt.

'We have looked everywhere for you,' said their Mother.

'And we found this on our travels,' said their Father holding a soggy piece of paper.

'Underneath your Christmas tree!
That is where you all should be!'

Betty and Bobby remembered that there was a Christmas tree very near their home and they raced towards it as fast as the snow would allow, with all the other animals following them.

It was nearly dark now and strange evening noises were filling Hazelnut Wood but their fears turned to excitement when, as the clue had suggested, they spotted the treasure chest under some branches in the snow. When they opened it they found presents for everybody inside.

Mr and Mrs Rabbit and Mrs Squirrel, who were waiting for them, had been getting a little worried, but they smiled when they looked through the window to see the happy faces coming towards them, Bobby and Simon carrying chest of presents. Mr Rabbit came outside with a lantern to greet them.

21

There was so much excitement over the many adventures that all the young animals tried to talk at once and there was much confusion and great joy as they all opened their presents.

Mrs Rabbit invited the Mouse family to have some tea and they all sat down to Christmas cake, fizzy lemonade, buns, scones and of course, hazelnuts.

Mr Rabbit was cheered for making up the Treasure Hunt.

Mr Squirrel was cheered for joining in and helping the younger ones.

Mr and Mrs Mouse were cheered for finding the last clue.

Those who stayed behind were cheered for preparing the scrumptious tea.

23

Eventually the weary families of mice and squirrels got up to leave.

Mrs Mouse thanked Mr Squirrel very much for rescuing Tommy and Tilly and they all thanked the Rabbits for giving them such a Happy Christmas Day.

'Look! It is starting to snow again,' said Simon.

'Hooray! Goodbye and thank you,' they all said, each wishing that perhaps next year they might share another exciting . . . . .

TREASURE HUNT.